Buster Baxter,
Cat Saver

A Marc Brown ARTHUR Chapter Book

Buster Baxter, Cat Saver

Text by Stephen Krensky
Based on a teleplay by Joe Fallon

Little, Brown and Company
Boston   New York   London

First Edition

The characters and events portrayed in this book are fictitious. Any
similarity to real persons, living or dead, is coincidental and not intended
by the author.

Arthur® is a registered trademark of Marc Brown.

Text has been reviewed and assigned a reading level by Laurel S. Ernst,
M.A., Teachers College, Columbia University, New York, New York;
reading specialist, Chappaqua, New York

Library of Congress Cataloging-in-Publication Data

Krensky, Stephen.
    Buster Baxter, cat saver / text by Stephen Krensky ; based on a
teleplay by Joe Fallon. — 1st ed.
        p.   cm. — (A Marc Brown Arthur chapter book ; 19)
    Summary: When Buster rescues a cat stuck in a tree he is treated like
a hero, but when he begins to enjoy his celebrity a little too much, his
friends devise a plan to bring him back to his old self.
    ISBN 0-316-12111-8 (hc) — ISBN 0-316-11817-6 (pb)
    [1. Fame Fiction.   2. Schools Fiction.   3. Aardvark Fiction.   4.
Animals Fiction.]   I. Fallon, Joe.   II. Title.   III. Series: Brown, Marc
Tolon. Marc Brown Arthur chapter book ; 19.
PZ7.K883B1   2000
[Fic] — dc21   99-42427

10 9 8 7 6 5 4 3 2

LAKE (hc)
COM-MO (pb)

Printed in the United States of America

For all my Cinar friends

Chapter 1

• • • • • • • • • • •

"What about Chocolate Chicken Crunch?"

"I don't think so," said Arthur.

He and Buster were standing at the counter inside the ice-cream shop. Arthur never had trouble choosing a flavor because he always ordered the same thing — chocolate. Buster, however, was much braver about trying something new.

"Well, I'm going to try it," said Buster. "I like chocolate. I like chicken. And I like crunchy things. So how bad can it be?"

Arthur shook his head. "I don't know," he said. "I'm just wondering what makes the crunch."

Buster just shrugged. The Brain's mother, who worked in the store, handed him his cone.

"An excellent choice," she said. "You're on the cutting edge, Buster. You're pushing the envelope. You're boldly going where —"

Buster took a lick. "Hmmmmm . . . Not bad."

"If you like that," said the Brain's mother, "you might want to try another one I'm experimenting with. I call it Peppermint Pasta."

"Sounds good!"

Buster took a spoonful and sucked down some spaghetti-like strands.

"I like it. But it's still missing something."

"Any suggestions?"

Buster suddenly smiled. "I know, I know — meatballs!"

"I'll keep that in mind. I have one more if you're interested. I'm calling it Rocky Trout."

"A fishy ice cream?" said Arthur.

"High in niacin and twelve essential vitamins," the Brain's mother explained. "When it comes to nutrition, you can't get more efficient than this."

"What's in it?" asked Arthur.

"Chocolate ice cream, almonds, and breaded fish sticks."

Arthur made a face. "Breaded fish sticks," he repeated.

Buster, however, was curious. He took a big bite and rolled it around in his mouth.

"Don't worry, Buster," said Arthur. "The hospital's close by. An ambulance can be here in no time if you need it."

Buster laughed. "It's great!" he said, giving the Brain's mother a big thumbs-up.

"You're brave to try so many new flavors," she told him.

Buster beamed. "You really think so?"

"Absolutely."

"And having a stainless-steel stomach doesn't hurt," Arthur added.

As they walked home, Buster offered Arthur a lick.

"You really should try some," he said. "The fish sticks are cooked just right."

Arthur's face turned a little green. "I'm glad to hear it, but I'm saving room for dinner."

Buster paused. "Do you really think I'm brave?" he asked.

Arthur shrugged. "I don't know."

"Well, thanks a lot!"

"Buster, I didn't mean it like that. I don't even know if I'm brave."

"You must be," said Buster. "D.W. is your sister, and you're still alive after all this time."

"True," said Arthur. "But I could be lucky, too. Being brave is different. You have to do the right thing in a dangerous or scary situation. You can't really predict what you'll do at a time like that until it actually happens."

"Can I tell you a secret, Arthur?"

"Of course."

Buster took a deep breath. "I wasn't brave when I was little. I always heard strange noises under my bed at night. And I got nervous just thinking about climbing a tree."

"But those things don't bother you anymore, right?"

Buster sighed. "I guess not. But to be safe," he added, "I take a quick look under my bed every night."

Chapter 2

· · · · · · · · · · ·

Buster was almost home when he came
upon a woman prancing around the base
of a huge tree.

"Why are you dancing?" Buster asked,
taking another lick of his cone.

"I'm not dancing," said the woman.
"I'm upset. It's my kitty — he's stuck in
the tree."

Buster looked up. There, in the top
branches, a small kitten was trembling.

"Don't fall, Alphonse!" said the woman.
She looked at Buster. "Can you help him?"

Buster frowned. There were no low

branches he could climb. Besides, Alphonse was up pretty high.

Buster took another lick of his cone. He wished there was more ice cream left. It would help him think.

A passing breeze drifted by him. It swirled round the ice cream, carrying the fishy smell up into the tree.

"This is terrible, just terrible," said the woman as she threw her hands into the air. "I need help, but I'm afraid to leave. What will happen to my kitty if I do go?" She squeezed her hands together. "Something must be done!"

"Don't worry," said Buster. "Such a little cat must still have all of its nine lives. So he'll probably be all right. Anyway, cats have too much sense to —"

"Look out!" cried the woman.

The kitten had gotten a good whiff of Buster's Rocky Trout and wanted to try it as soon as possible. The quickest way was straight down, and so the kitten leaped off the branch and fell through the air toward Buster.

"Alphonse!" screeched the woman.

Before Buster could think of anything to do or say, the kitten landed in his arms. There, it immediately began eating the ends of the fish sticks out of Buster's cone.

"Hey!" cried Buster. "That's my ice cream you're eating."

The kitten didn't seem to care. Buster might have said more, but the prancing woman was now shaking his hand.

"Thank you, thank you, thank you!" she cried. "You saved Alphonse!"

Buster didn't know what to say. "Well, I . . ."

"Don't be so modest. It was very brave of you to jump in like that. Other boys might not have done so."

"It wasn't really . . ." Buster blinked. "Did you say *brave*?"

"Of course." The woman picked up Alphonse, who had finished off the last of the fish sticks. "You're a hero. In fact, this is just the kind of news we need to see more of in the newspaper."

Buster was slowly turning red. "You're kidding, right?"

"I certainly am not, young man. What's your name?"

"Buster. Buster Baxter."

"Buster Baxter," she repeated. "What a fine name for a hero. Come with me!"

"Where are we going?"

"We're marching down to the newspaper this minute. Your deed should not go unmarked."

"My mother works at the newspaper," said Buster.

"Then she will soon be very proud of you. And when I get done, the rest of the world will be proud of you, too."

Chapter 3

• • • • • • • • • • • •

When Arthur got home, D.W. was dancing around a boom box on the den floor. A song was playing loudly.

> *"Crazy bus, crazy bus,*
> *Riding on the crazy bus."*

"D.W.," said Arthur, "can I ask you a question?"

"Not now, Arthur. Can't you see I'm busy?"

"Busy? How can you say that? You've played this song . . . ," he said, as he moved over to a blackboard covered in hash marks and added up the groups of five, ". . . three hundred and seventy-five times since Monday."

D.W. smiled. "I know. Probably a new world record, don't you think?"

> *"Driving up, driving down,*
> *In the country, back in town,*
> *Wacky, gooney, goofy, spooney,*
> *High as a plane or balloon-y."*

"Balloon-y?" said Arthur. "What kind of word is that?"

D.W. ignored him and kept singing along.

> *"Crazy bus, come with us,*
> *Dopey, doofy, screwy, blue-y,*
> *Gooey, chewy, fooey, dewey,*
> *Absolutely bus-a-looey*
> *Crazy, lazy, crazy, crazy bus*
> *Crazy — bus — crazy!"*

The song ended.

"Finally," said Arthur. "It's over. Now you can answer my question."

D.W. folded her arms. "You have thirty seconds while the tape is rewinding."

"Fine," said Arthur. "I just wanted to know . . . Do you think I'm brave?"

"Brave? You? Come on, what's the real question?"

"That's it. Honest."

D.W. started to laugh. And once she started, she couldn't stop. She clutched her sides helplessly and rolled onto the floor.

"You? Ha ha ha. Brave? Oh, that's a good one. No, a great one. Brave Arthur. Ha ha ha ha!"

"A simple 'no' would have been enough," said Arthur, stomping out of the room.

Out on the porch, Arthur sat down with Pal.

"You think I'm brave, don't you, boy?"

Pal wagged his tail.

"Good dog!"

"In fact," Arthur went on, "I'm probably about the bravest person you know. Right, Pal?"

Pal moaned and lay down at Arthur's feet.

"You're right," said Arthur. "I should quit while I'm ahead."

They sat there quietly for a while. A newspaper boy rode by and threw the evening paper up the walk.

Arthur walked over to get it. "I'll read the funnies to you, boy."

Pal barked.

Arthur opened the paper and looked at the headline.

BOY HERO CATCHES CAT

"That's Buster!" he shouted. "Look, Pal! It's Buster!"

Pal barked.

"This is amazing. He's on the front page and everything."

Arthur jumped up and ran into the garage.

"Buster's a hero!" he told his father, who was loading trays of cookies into his van.

"If you say so."

"He is, he is!" Arthur insisted, continuing into the house.

"Buster's a hero!" he announced to his mother, who was hunched over the computer.

"That's nice, dear."

Arthur even poked his head into the den, where D.W. was still dancing.

"Buster's a hero!" he shouted over the lyrics.

"Don't get me started again," said D.W., holding her sides. "I'm all laughed out."

"But it's true. See for yourself." He showed D.W. the front page.

17

"Well," she said, surprised for once. "Imagine that."

Chapter 4

. . . .

At school the next morning, all the kids were gathered around Buster.

"It was no big deal, really," said Buster. "I was just in the right place at the right time."

"You're too modest, Buster," said Muffy.

"True," the Brain insisted. "You showed great presence of mind. You really had to think on your feet."

Buster blushed.

"What's the matter?" asked Francine. "Cat got your tongue?"

Everyone laughed.

The crowd suddenly parted as Binky pushed in from the back.

"So you're a big hero, huh?" he said, towering over Buster.

Everyone shifted uncomfortably.

"Well," said Buster, "that's what people are saying."

"Yeah, that's what I heard. So I was wondering . . ."

"Yes?" Buster squeaked.

Binky took a deep breath. "Can I have your autograph?"

He held out a piece of paper.

Later, at a special school assembly, the principal, Mr. Haney, stood at the podium.

"It's not often that we get the chance to honor one of our own students at Lakewood Elementary. But today we have that pleasure. Let's give a big round of applause to a special hero — Buster Baxter!"

As the students cheered, Buster shyly

stepped up to the microphone.

"Testing, testing . . . Is this thing on?"

"Any words of wisdom for your classmates?" Mr. Haney asked.

Buster paused. "I was just doing my best," he said.

Everyone cheered again.

On the way home with Arthur, Buster couldn't stop talking. "You wouldn't believe what a day I've had. Everyone's been so nice to me. Sue Ellen offered to give me batting lessons. And Muffy actually gave me a cream puff at lunch."

"The kind with the rainbow sprinkles?"

Buster nodded.

Arthur looked impressed. "Wow! Muffy never shares those with anyone."

As they continued walking, Arthur noticed people stopping to point at Buster.

"It's him! The cat saver!"

"The kid hero!"

"Amazing!" said Arthur. "Everybody knows you."

"You think so?"

Buster waved to the passing crowd; they waved back.

"Hey, you're right."

At the ice-cream shop, there was a special on a flavor named after Buster.

"See that?" said Buster. "Just for me!" There was also a sign — BUSTER EATS HERE — in the window.

"It's like a dream," said Buster. "But even better."

"Why is it better?" asked Arthur.

"Because," said Buster, "it's real."

The "dream" continued the next day when a reporter and a photographer showed up at school.

"They're doing a follow-up story," Buster explained to Arthur. He turned to the photographer. "Get a picture of me with my fans — uh, I mean classmates."

During recess, the reporter stood with a tape recorder as Buster told the story again. Arthur, Francine, and Binky were listening.

"Then," said Buster, "the helicopter lowered me toward the kitty. I had to leap with precision and timing, risking my very life!"

"I'm getting a little tired of this story," said Francine.

"Not me," said Binky. "It's different every time. This is the first I've heard of the helicopter."

Arthur had noticed that, too. The story was changing, becoming bigger and grander with each retelling. Arthur was glad Buster was enjoying his big moment in the sun. But he couldn't help feeling that clouds were gathering on the horizon.

Chapter 5

• • • • • • • • • • •

"You don't look very happy, Arthur," said Mr. Read, turning on the oven.

Arthur looked up from the kitchen table, which he was setting for dinner.

"Now, I realize," his father continued, "that setting the table is probably not your favorite activity. But I think something else is bothering you."

"How can you tell?"

"Well, for one thing, you put all the forks upside down."

Arthur stared at the table. He had done just that.

"It's Buster," he said, turning the forks around.

"Ah, our local hero. He's certainly getting a lot of attention."

"I don't mind that," said Arthur. "I'm happy for him. But all the attention has changed Buster. He's different."

"Are you the only one who's noticed?"

Arthur shook his head. "Oh, no. The whole class has noticed. In fact, everyone is mad at him because he's acting like such a big shot."

Mr. Read took a chicken out of the refrigerator. "What has he done exactly?"

"Well, when we went to the movie theater yesterday, there was a long line. I figured we would go to the end as usual. Not Buster. He pulled me past everyone all the way to the front. I told him we couldn't just cut like that. He just laughed and pulled out his picture from the newspaper.

'I'm Buster Baxter!' he told everyone. '*The* Buster Baxter.' "

"Then what happened?" asked Mr. Read.

"The kids in line grumbled a little, although nobody actually complained out loud. But then the usher gave Buster a big salute and waved him through.

" 'I told you so,' Buster said to me. I mentioned that everyone was mad because we had cut in line. He just shrugged. 'I'm a hero, Arthur. Heroes always get cuts.' "

Mr. Read lightly coated the chicken in olive oil, sprinkled on some garlic salt, and placed it in the oven. "What else have you noticed?"

"He told the Brain to start doing his homework for him."

Mr. Read laughed. "What did the Brain say to that?"

"He asked Buster why. And Buster explained that he was going to be very busy patrolling the neighborhood and looking out for other cats in trouble."

Mr. Read sighed. "I once had a friend who did almost the same thing. He put out a fire that had been accidentally started in the woods. The firemen made a big deal about it and let him ride around on their truck and use the siren. He was getting plenty of compliments, too. Pretty soon he started thinking he was too hot to handle."

"What happened in the end?"

"A bunch of kids ambushed him with pails of water. That finally cooled him off. But it was also embarrassing. I was always sorry that I hadn't spoken to him sooner. It might have made a difference. And I was his friend, after all."

Athur looked at the floor. "Do you think I should talk to Buster?"

"You have to decide that for yourself. But I will say one thing: Being someone's friend isn't always easy."

Arthur nodded. "That's for sure," he said.

Chapter 6

· · · · · · · · · · · ·

"I'm glad you asked me over," Arthur told Buster. "We need to talk."

They were standing in Buster's room. It was messier than usual because, as Buster had explained, heroes don't clean up after themselves.

"Buster, can I tell you something?"

"Look at this first," said Buster, pulling some papers from under his bed.

Arthur looked at the first page. "*Cat Saver*?" he said.

"It's the TV show I'm writing. It's based on my own true-life adventures."

"Adventures? Buster, you've only had one adventure."

Buster ignored this. "Naturally," he went on, "I'll be the star. Which is only right because all famous heroes end up on TV."

"Buster, I really think we should —"

"Wait, listen to this." Buster cleared his throat.

"Our story begins in a top secret headquarters. . . .

Buster stood before a giant video screen surrounded by a lot of computers.

There was a knock at the door.

'Come in,' said Buster.

A woman entered. 'Thank goodness I found you, Cat Saver. Can you rescue my car?'

'Yes, I — Wait a minute. Your car? Not your cat?'

She nodded. 'You're my last hope.'

Buster thought about it. 'Is your car up a tree?'

'Yes. That's why I thought of you.'

'Hmmmm,' said Buster, 'a car up a tree. That would be a challenge. . . .'

'Please! I fear my car has little time left before it's too late.'

Buster jumped up. 'Then,' he declared, 'we haven't a moment to lose.'

He leaped over to a tuba standing on end nearby. He blew into the mouthpiece and a costume flew out and enveloped him. Topped by a shirt with the symbol of a cat in a tree, the costume included power gloves and big jumping boots.

A roar filled the room as jets in the bottom of the jumping boots lifted Buster into the air.

'I'm on my way,' he shouted, before crashing through the window.

But when Buster reached the tree, there was no car in sight.

'No sign of a struggle or tire marks — and yet the car is gone. It must be a trap.'

'That's right!' said the woman, who had

followed him in a motorized cat-litter box. She pulled off her disguise to reveal herself as the evil Catnapper. 'I had to get you out of your lair. Now we will deal with you once and for all!'

'We?' said Buster.

Catnapper clawed at the air and her two masked assistants came out of hiding. Cat Saver looked them over.

'All right, you evil fur balls,' he said, 'let's see what you're made of!' "

"Okay, Buster," said Arthur, "I get the idea."

"Cat Saver knew this battle would be a hard one. He —"

"BUSTER!"

Buster took a deep breath. "Sorry, I just like getting into the part. So, what do you think?"

"What do I think?" Arthur sighed. "I'll tell you what I think. Everybody's tired of all this hero stuff. Really tired."

Buster was silent for a moment. "Well," he said, "I never expected this from you."

"Expected what?"

"That you'd be jealous."

"Me? Jealous? What makes you say that?"

Buster just smiled. "A hero," he said, "can always tell."

Chapter 7

• • • • • • • • • • •

Arthur sat in the tree house with Francine and the Brain.

"So what did Buster say?" Francine asked.

"First, he said I was jealous. I tried to explain to him that very few TV shows actually get made and that none had ever been written by a kid about himself."

"What did he say to that?" asked Francine.

"That it was about time the situation changed, and that he was just the person to make it happen."

"He's certainly got the confidence part down," the Brain admitted.

"He also told me I'd be invited to all the cast parties, so I wouldn't feel left out."

Francine frowned. "What about us? I'd like to go to a cast party, too."

"Francine . . ."

"There could be famous stars there, sipping those drinks with the little umbrellas."

"Francine . . ."

"And talent scouts." Francine patted her hair. "I could be discovered, maybe even get my own show —"

"FRANCINE!" the Brain shouted. "This isn't really going to happen, remember?"

"But, still . . ."

The Brain went on, "Did Buster have any other reaons he thought his show would be a success?"

"Well," said Arthur, "he explained that

the concept would be a new form of *edutainment*."

"Edutainment?" Francine repeated. "Is that really a word?"

Arthur shrugged. "It is according to Buster."

"The idea is supposed to be a mixture of education and entertainment," the Brain explained. "Often, though, it's the worst parts of both."

Arthur shook his head. "Not to Buster," he said.

"Then this problem is worse than I thought," said the Brain. "We have to get Buster to understand what he's doing. A lot of the kids are already complaining. If he keeps it up, soon nobody will be talking to him."

Francine sighed. "And it's not like he saved the world or anything. I mean, a kitten is important, but . . ."

"I know, I know," said Arthur. "But just for a minute, pretend you're Buster. He's never had a chance to look special, to have people *oohing* and *ahhing* over him. This is his moment — even if he has gone a little overboard."

"What if we all talked to him together?" said the Brain.

Arthur watched a spider spinning its web in the corner of the tree house. "I don't think he'll listen. He'll just say we're all jealous."

"In that case," said Francine, "we'll have to teach him a lesson. We need to make him realize that he's not quite as much of a hero as he thinks."

Arthur brightened. "I have an idea," he said. "If Buster was just lucky the first time, then he wouldn't know what to do if he had to save a cat again."

"True," said the Brain, "but what are the odds of Buster being around when another cat gets stuck in a tree?" He paused and then smiled. "Oh, I see, we're going to give the odds a little help. But what if Buster succeeds this time, too?"

Arthur sighed. "We'll just have to take that chance."

Chapter 8

• • • • • • • • • • •

A little later, Buster walked down the street with a reporter and a photographer hurrying alongside him.

"So what are your future plans?" asked the reporter. "There have been rumors you may run for president."

"I don't think so." said Buster. "I don't want to be tied down like that. But to answer the question, I'll still save the occasional cat, of course. It's important to stay close to your roots. But my real future is in TV. I have a mission, to spread —"

"Buster! Buster!" shouted Arthur and Francine, running up to him.

"What's up?" asked Buster. "And try to stay calm. Count to ten."

"Never mind that," said Francine. "This is an emergency."

"There's a cat in trouble," said Arthur. "Look!"

He pointed high up into a tree.

Buster squinted upward. "I don't see anything."

"It's right there," said Francine.

Turning to the bushes, Arthur gave a signal.

The Brain, who was hidden there, pressed a button on a remote control. Then, high up in the tree, a plastic cat made a sound.

"Meow!"

"Did you hear that?" asked Francine.

"It's the cat!" said Arthur.

"A cat in trouble," Francine added. "Thank goodness you're here."

"That was really a cat?" said Buster.

"Of course," Arthur insisted. "What else would it be?"

"Well, it didn't sound quite right."

"Naturally," said Arthur. "You wouldn't sound right, either, if you were trapped high up in a tree."

"Meow! Meow!"

"Come on, Buster," said Francine. "Do something!"

"Why don't *you* do something?" Buster asked.

Arthur and Francine looked at him with surprise.

"You're the hero, Buster," said Francine. "Remember?"

Buster nodded. "Right, right, of course."

The reporter held up her microphone. "Ladies and gentlemen, watch as history repeats itself. Our young hero, Buster, is going to save another cat, and we're here, live on the scene."

The photographer moved all around,

snapping pictures of the historic moment.

"No flash pictures, please," Buster told him, holding up his hand. "I need to, um, concentrate."

"Meow, meow, meow!"

"What are you waiting for?" Francine asked. "After all, you know how to save a cat."

Buster sighed. "Here, kitty, kitty . . . ," he whispered. He wiped the sweat from his forehead. "Buster will save you. Come on, kitty. . . ."

"You can do more than that," said Arthur. "Don't leave it all up to the cat. We want to see you be a hero."

Buster started shaking. "All right, all right, I admit it. I'm not sure what to do."

The photographer stopped snapping pictures and stared at Buster.

"I got lucky before. I was in the right place at the right time."

"Whoa!" said the reporter. "Hold the

front page. This story has taken an unex-
pected turn."

A sudden breeze blew by, swaying the
branches overhead.

Francine glanced up. "Look out!" she
cried.

Something was falling down through
the branches. Buster reached out his arms,
but a final gust blew the plastic cat away
from his outstretched fingers. It fell at his
feet — and smashed into bits.

Chapter 9

• • • • • • • • • • • •

The reporter stared at the ground.

"A dangerous situation has come to a tragic conclusion," she stated gravely.

The photographer started snapping pictures.

Buster stared at the plastic pieces at his feet. "That's not a cat!" he cried. "At least not a real cat!"

"Are you sure?" asked Francine. "You know, some cats are pretty unusual. Siamese, Manx . . ."

Buster hesitated for a moment. Then he shook his head. He pointed his finger at Arthur and Francine. "This was a setup.

You two faked this whole thing to make fun of me."

"We did not!" Francine insisted.

"Well, then to make me look bad."

"In the face of a disaster," the reporter continued, "there is always plenty of blame to go around. And sometimes, the finger-pointing can get quite ugly."

"We didn't want to make you look bad," said Arthur. "But you wouldn't listen to me. We just wanted to get your attention. Buster, we're proud that you're our friend and that you saved the cat, but you've gone too far." He took a deep breath. "I wish there was another way to say this, but everyone's tired of you bragging and acting like such a big shot."

Buster started to speak, but no words came out. He looked down at the remains of the plastic cat and then back up into the tree. "Okay, okay. You're right. I'm sorry I acted that way. Will you forgive me?"

Arthur folded his arms. "What about the TV show?"

Buster bit his lip. "I have to give that up, too? Boy, you guys are tough."

Arthur stared at him.

"All right, all right," said Buster.

"As the TV show fades to black," said the reporter, "only the possible presidential campaign remains."

"Forget about that, too," Buster told her. "Too much work." He put a hand across his chest. "If nominated, I will not run. If elected, I will not serve. I am not — Look out! Runaway piano!"

"Very funny," said Francine.

"Trying to get back at us, eh?" said Arthur. "Really, Buster, you can do better than that. We're not falling for that old runaway piano tri— aaghh!"

Buster dove at Francine and Arthur, pushing them onto the grass.

"Hey!" Francine shouted.

A huge piano rolled past them. If Francine and Arthur had stayed where they had been, they would have been flatter than a leaky tire.

"That was close," said Buster. "Too close."

Two piano movers came huffing and puffing down the street. They were gaining on the piano, but slowly.

"Sorry!" shouted the movers as they ran past.

Arthur and Francine shared a look.

"We would have been crushed!" said Arthur.

"Very crushed," said Francine. "Buster saved us!"

The photographer moved in for a picture as a crowd gathered.

"News is where you find it," said the reporter. "And we just found it big time. Buster Baxter, you've done it again. What are your thoughts, your heroic thoughts, at a moment like this?"

"I'm glad you asked," said Buster, putting his hands on his hips and sticking out his chest as far as possible.

"Oh, no," muttered Arthur. "Here we go again!"

Chapter 10

• • • • • • • • • • • •

"High above an unsuspecting city, a piano fell out an apartment window.

A woman stuck her head out after it. 'Look out below!' she yelled.

As the piano fell toward the street, the people on the sidewalk looked up, frozen in terror.

'There's no time to escape.'

'We're doomed!'

Suddenly, a costumed figure jetted across the sky on rocket roller skates. His metallic battle suit gleamed in the sunlight.

'When pianos run amuck, I spring into action. And who am I? Buster Baxter, Piano

Tamer! Now you'll have to excuse me, I have a job to do.'

In the blink of an eye, Buster dove toward the falling piano, catching it just moments before it crushed a sidewalk full of people.

'Anyone can save a cat, but only one hero can tame a wild piano without hitting a false note.' "

"You're kidding, right?" said Arthur.

Buster looked up from his notes and flexed his muscles. "It would make a great movie. I see a costume with all eighty-eight keys going around my chest and back."

"I don't think so."

"It would be great."

"No way."

"How about a CD?"

"Dream on."

Buster paused. "A tape? Can I have a tape?"

Arthur kept walking. "Buster, you've shown you're a hero. You should be happy with that."

"It's a good start," Buster admitted. "But I want more. What about an exercise video?"

Arthur just shook his head.

"A comic strip inside a pack of gum? Come on, Arthur, give me a break."

Arthur kept on walking. When Buster got something into his head, he held on tight. His bravery might come and go, but one thing was certain.

His stubbornness was forever.